Karen's Epilepsy

Written and Illustrated by
Elizabeth Baltaro

Published by:

Boutique of Quality Books Publishing Company

www.bqbpublishing.com

Printed in the United States of America

ISBN 978-1-60808-015-1 (p)
ISBN 978-1-60808-110-3 (e)

For children everywhere with epilepsy.

When Karen's parents told her they would be moving in the summer, Karen was very upset. She did not want to move from her home in California. She liked her friends and her school very much. She did not want to leave them behind. Most of all, she dreaded having to be "the new kid."

"Mom, why do we have to move?" Karen asked one night at the dinner table.

“Because your father has found a new job,” her mother replied between bites.

“I wish daddy had never found a new job!” Karen yelled.

She left the table and went to her room. She began to cry, because she was scared. She didn't want to have to make new friends or have new neighbors.

She was scared most of all because she had epilepsy, a seizure disorder. A few times a week she would have a seizure. Sometimes, when she had a seizure, Karen would walk around and make noises for a few minutes. She did not really know what she did when she had a seizure, because she couldn't think, hear, or see what she was doing. Karen had to take medicine everyday, but she still had seizures.

Karen's type of seizure was called a complex partial seizure. There were other kinds of seizures, too. Almost anything someone can do in real life, they can do in a seizure. Karen knew a lot about epilepsy, and so did her friends and her teachers. They had grown up with her. She was scared of moving someplace where nobody knew anything about her seizures. What if the kids at her new school made fun of her because she was different? Karen wouldn't know what to do.

“We’ll show them a video about seizures, and I’ll talk to all your new teachers about you, Honey. Everything will be fine,” Karen’s mother assured her, but Karen knew everything would not be fine.

Too soon, the school year ended. Karen hugged all her teachers and told them how much she would miss them. Her mom let her have a special party to say goodbye to all her friends. All the dinner plates and silverware were packed in boxes, so they had to eat on paper plates. Karen said good-bye to everyone at the end of the party. Then she went to her room and sat all by herself.

She liked her room a lot. It hardly seemed like her room anymore. The walls were bare, and her toys were all in boxes. She knew she wouldn't like her room at the new house as much as this room.

When Karen saw the new house, she told her mom it was ugly, but she really thought it was beautiful. It was brown with a pointed tower on the right side. It had a big bay window and a small front porch. Karen's new room had two windows. It was bigger than her old room. She had a walk-in closet. She looked out of her window into the backyard. There was a tall tree that grew near her window. She loved her new room. Karen's parents peeked in to see how she was doing. Karen was startled when she saw their reflection in the window.

"How do you like your new room?" Karen's father asked.

"I hate it!" Karen said, angrily.

"Oh, I see...well, there is a girl from your new school who has invited you to her house. She lives very close, and she will be in your class," Karen's father said.

"No! I don't want to meet anybody new," Karen yelled.

"Ok. We just thought you'd like to make a few friends before school started," Karen's father replied.

"Fine. I guess I'll go," Karen whispered.

"Good," said Karen's dad, "We'll drive you there this afternoon."

“We got you something we would like you to wear,” Karen’s mom said holding out a silver bracelet. Karen thought it was beautiful. It had a charm with a red cross engraved in it. Then she read the charm. It said, “EPILEPSY.”

“I don’t want to wear THAT! Then everyone will know I have epilepsy,” she cried.

“Karen, we know it’s hard for you, but we think you would be safer if you wore this bracelet,” Karen’s mom pleaded, so Karen let her mother clip the bracelet on her wrist.

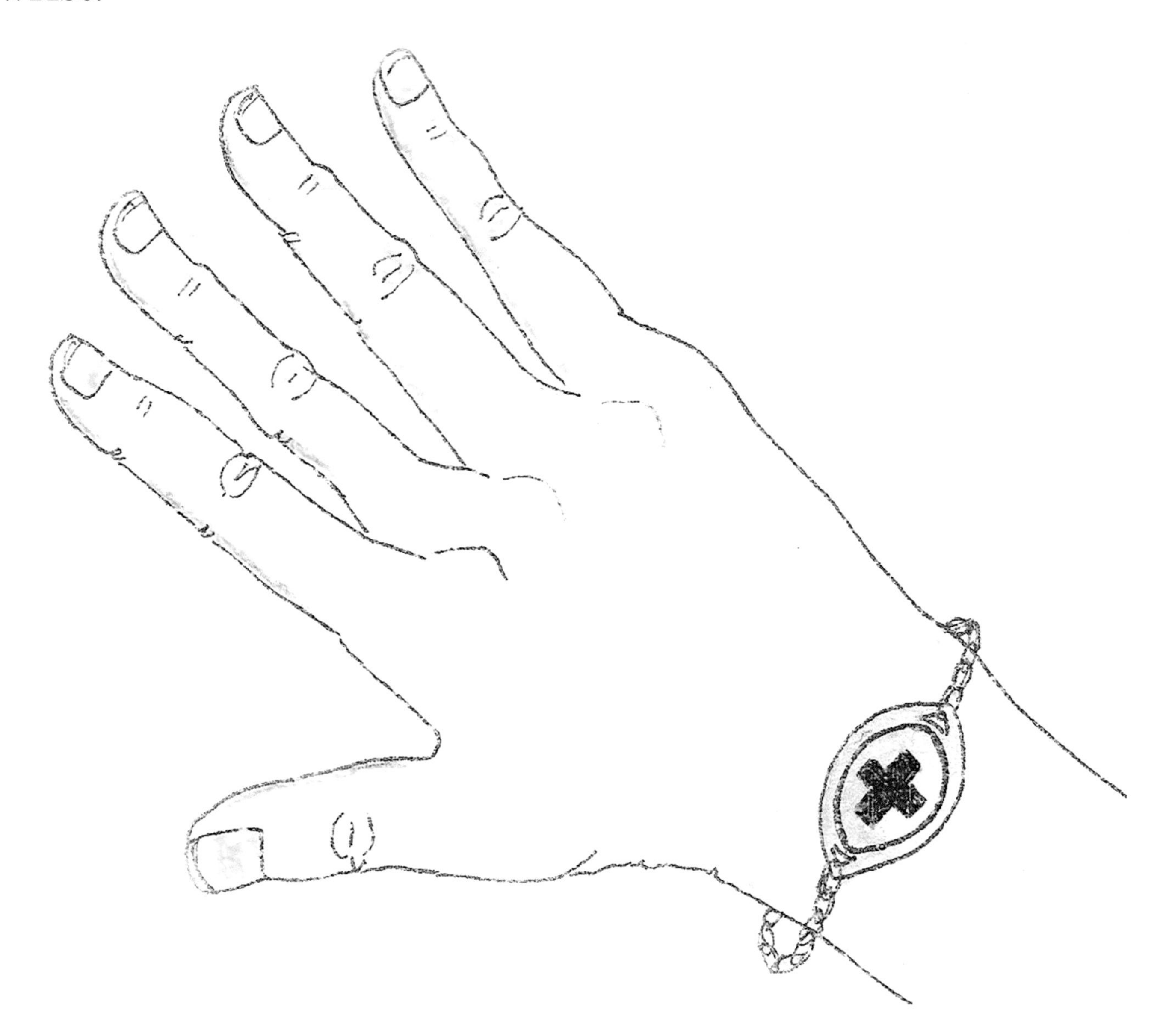

That afternoon Karen put on a long-sleeved shirt to wear to the new girl's house. She did not want anyone to see her new bracelet.

When she arrived at the new house, she saw a girl in the front yard waiting for her. She had blonde hair. She was wearing a T-shirt and shorts, because it was hot outside. Karen was burning up in her long-sleeved shirt, but she didn't say anything. Karen's dad left her with the new girl.

"My name is Anne," the girl said quietly, "What's yours?"

"My name is Karen," Karen squeaked.

"Aren't you hot?" Anne asked Karen, noticing her long sleeves.

"Yes," Karen said.

"Want to go inside?" Anne asked.

"Sure."

They played for a little while, and Karen had fun. Then, Anne asked if Karen wanted to go swimming. Karen said no, even though she wanted to. She was scared she might have a seizure in the pool, and Anne wouldn't know what to do. When Karen left, she told Anne she would see her on the first day of school.

On the first day of school, Karen was very nervous. She found her classroom and her new teacher, Mrs. Jenkins. Mrs. Jenkins was nice to Karen.

"If you need any help, just ask me," Mrs. Jenkins told Karen.

However, during the morning, Karen suddenly heard tapping in her left ear. It was inside her ear. She knew what this tapping meant. She was going to have a seizure. Karen raised her hand, but Mrs. Jenkins did not call on her. Then Karen could not see or hear anything. Karen walked around the room, made funny sounds, and drooled. Many of the kids laughed at Karen. Mrs. Jenkins knew what was happening and made sure Karen did not walk into anything dangerous.

After a minute or two, Karen stopped, and she could see everyone again. She was confused and couldn't remember exactly where she was at first or why everyone was staring at her. Then she remembered that she had had a seizure. Karen felt terrible. She was tired and felt like crying. Mrs. Jenkins explained to the class that Karen had epilepsy, and the seizure was normal for her. However, the children treated her differently.

At lunch, nobody sat by Karen, so she ate all by herself. At recess, she leaned against a brick wall instead of playing. Nobody asked her to play any games. Even Anne was too scared to ask Karen to play with her. Some boys from her class walked up to Karen and pretended to have a seizure. They walked around her and made silly noises and spit on the ground.

“Stop it!” she yelled, “Leave me alone!” She thought of her friends at her old school. She missed them a lot. They would never make fun of her.

That afternoon, when her mom picked her up, Karen started to cry.

"What happened, Karen?" her mom asked.

"I had a seizure this morning," Karen sobbed.

"Yes, I know. The school called and told me."

"Nobody likes me. They think I'm weird."

"Do you want me to give your teacher the movie to show your classmates about seizures?" Karen's mom asked.

"No! I don't want them to know anything about it. Then, they'll hate me even more," Karen cried.

"Things will get better," Karen's mom assured her.

Karen went to school everyday for several weeks, and things did not improve at all. She was very unhappy with her new school. The only person she liked was Mrs. Jenkins.

At the end of September, something very important happened. The day began for Karen similar to all the other school days. It was dull and boring. She ate lunch and during recess stood all by herself. After lunch, Mrs. Jenkins did not look as though she felt well.

“Boys and girls, I am not feeling well. I am going to go home for the afternoon, and Mrs. Stevens, the principal, will teach....” Mrs. Jenkins stopped and fell on the floor. She began to shake. Many of the children were afraid, and they didn’t know what to do.

“Mrs. Jenkins is having a seizure!” Karen yelled. “Somebody go get the principal!” Karen went up to Mrs. Jenkins. She knew exactly what to do. She carefully turned Mrs. Jenkins’ head so it was facing sideways. Mrs. Jenkins would be able to breathe easier in this position. Then, Karen put a jacket underneath Mrs. Jenkins’ head so it would not bang on the hard floor.

“Don’t touch her. She might be contagious!” somebody yelled.

“No, seizures aren’t contagious,” Karen replied. Karen slowly removed the glasses Mrs. Jenkins was wearing and loosened the scarf around her neck. She moved away a chair that was near Mrs. Jenkins’ head so she wouldn’t hurt herself. Karen watched the clock on the wall. She knew it was important to know how long the seizure lasted.

By the time Principal Stevens and the school nurse came in, Mrs. Jenkins had stopped shaking hard. Karen went back to her seat, and the nurse examined Mrs. Jenkins. Mrs. Stevens explained to the class that everything would be all right. Mrs. Jenkins was finally able to stand up, but she looked pale.

“Well,” said the nurse, “Mrs. Jenkins needs to come with me, but it looks like she’ll be ok. It is a good thing someone knew what to do to help her.” The nurse helped Mrs. Jenkins out of the classroom.

“I think we all need to thank Karen for being so brave. It is very scary to have a seizure,” Mrs. Stevens said. Everyone in the class smiled at Karen and clapped.

After school, lots of kids wanted to talk to Karen.

"How did you know what to do?" one boy asked.

"I know a lot about different types of seizures, because I have epilepsy," Karen said, proudly. "If you want, I can bring in a movie about seizures sometime, and I can teach you all what to do."

"Yes!' they all shouted, enthusiastically. Maybe, things wouldn't be so bad anymore Karen thought. Then, Anne walked up to Karen.

"Why didn't you just tell me about epilepsy to begin with? If you had told me, I would have known why you acted so strangely. I thought it was because you didn't like me," said Anne.

"I thought you didn't like me!" Karen said, surprised by Anne's remark.

"No," said Anne, "I think you are very special!" They both laughed.